THIS

SWEET PICKLES ®

BOOK
BELONGS TO

In the Town of Sweet Pickles, the animals get
into and out of pickles because of their all too
human personality traits.

Each of the books in the *Sweet Pickles* series
is about a different pickle.

This story is about making
mistakes ... and fixing them.

Grolier Enterprises Inc. offers a varied selection of children's book racks and tote bags. For details on ordering, please write: Grolier Enterprises Inc., Sherman Turnpike, Danbury, CT 06816 Attn: Premium Department

Library of Congress Cataloging in Publication Data

Reinach, Jacquelyn.
    Wet paint.
    (Sweet Pickles)
    SUMMARY: Clever Camel disarms her accusers when she admits to making a mistake and offers to repair the damage she caused.
    [1. Camels—Fiction] I. Hefter, Richard. II. Perle, Ruth Lerner. III. Title. IV. Series.
PZ7.R2747We   [E]   81-4849
ISBN 0-937524-06-9   AACR2

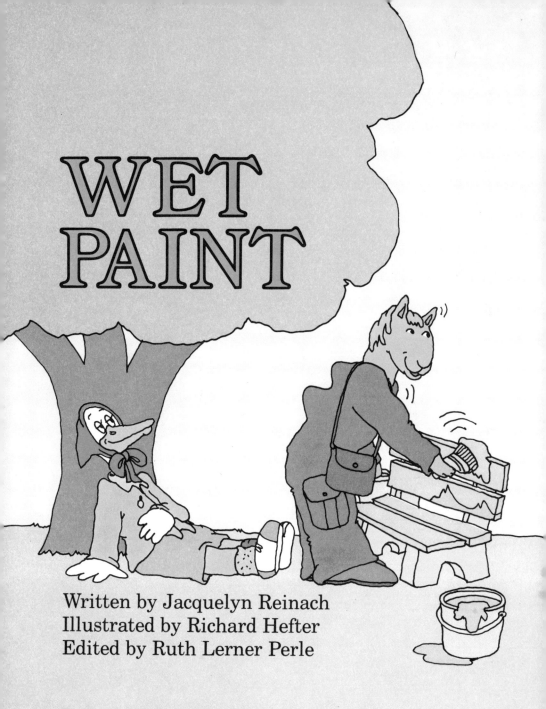

WET PAINT

Written by Jacquelyn Reinach
Illustrated by Richard Hefter
Edited by Ruth Lerner Perle

Euphrosyne Incorporated

It was a fine spring morning in the Town of Sweet Pickles.

Clever Camel was working in the park, painting the benches red, yellow and blue. Goof-Off Goose was resting under a tree, watching Camel paint.

Just then, Enormous Elephant came strolling down the path carrying a huge picnic basket. "Hi, there, Camel!" called Elephant. "I'm taking my morning cake break. Would you like to join me?"

"That would be nice," said Camel. "I'm almost finished, anyway."

Camel went off with Elephant, leaving her paint
cart where it was.

"Hey, Camel," sighed Goose, "you forgot to put up the
WET PAINT signs!"

But Camel was already out of sight. Goose yawned and went to sleep.

At noon, everybody came out to have lunch in the park. Jealous Jackal and Nasty Nightingale found a red bench and sat down. Imitating Iguana sat down, too.

Vain Vulture and Doubtful Dog stopped at a yellow bench. "This is the perfect place to have lunch," smiled Vulture. "The bench matches my new shirt perfectly ... all yellow and shiny!"

"That paint looks wet!" said Dog. "I doubt we should sit there."

"If the paint were wet," said Vulture, "Camel would have put up WET PAINT signs. Clever Camel never makes mistakes!" Vulture sat down.

"Well, all right," muttered Dog. He sat down.

Healthy Hippo and Accusing Alligator sat down on a blue bench. Hippo spread his lunch out neatly. "Would you like one of my carrots?" he said to Alligator. "It's full of vitamins!"

"Look at that carrot!" cried Alligator. "It's all *blue!* You didn't wash it! Are you trying to poison me?"

"I *always* wash my food before eating!" declared Hippo. He looked at the carrot. "Oh, my goodness!" he cried. "The carrot *is* blue! The paint on this bench is WET!"

"WHAT?" shouted Alligator.

"WET!" screamed Hippo. He jumped up.
"THE PAINT ON THIS BENCH IS WET!"

"WET PAINT!"

Everybody jumped up. Everybody's bottom was covered with paint ... red, yellow or blue.

"My clothes!" moaned Vulture. "My beautiful designer clothes are *ruined*!"

"Mine too!" moaned Iguana.

"BLECHH!" screeched Alligator, waving her sticky blue tail. "Someone is to blame for this and I want to know who!"

"Look!" called Hippo. "Here's Camel's painting cart with all of her stuff. And, look! Here's a whole stack of WET PAINT signs!"

"Ah ha!" shouted Alligator. "That proves it! This mess is all Camel's fault! She painted the benches and didn't put up the signs! She's the one to blame!"

"I'll get her for this!" yelled Jackal.

"Me too!" yelled Iguana.

"I'll bet Camel will have a million excuses!" sighed Dog. "She won't admit she did it!"

"Oh, she'd better admit it!" shouted Alligator. "I'll *get* her to admit it. I'll say, 'Listen, Camel, we know you did it. So admit it! Or else!'"

"Yeah!" growled Jackal. "And no excuses!"

"I can't believe Camel would *do* such a thing!" groaned Vulture. "Camel *always* does the right thing!"

"Oh, you think Miss Ever-Clever Camel is so perfect?" sneered Nightingale. "I bet she did it on purpose! Just to be MEAN! Nyaah!"

"I bet so too!" sneered Iguana. "Camel is MEAN!"

"...and JEALOUS!" yelled Jackal. "She's jealous because we're all having lunch in the park and she isn't!"

"I think so too!" yelled Iguana. "She's JEALOUS!"

"...and IRRESPONSIBLE!" cried Hippo.

"...and WEIRD!" cried Dog.

"...and MALICIOUS!" cried Vulture.

Everybody shouted and yelled.

"What are we waiting for?" screamed Alligator. "Let's go get Camel!"

"LET'S GET HER!" shouted everybody.

They all stormed down the path just as Camel was coming back.

"Ah ha!" cried Alligator, pointing at Camel. "There you are! We caught you! Don't try to squirm out of it! We know you're to blame!"

Camel saw everybody covered with paint.

"Oh, my!" she gasped. "I'm so sorry! I didn't get back in time to put up the WET PAINT signs. Now you're all messed up and it's my fault!"

"WHAT?" shouted Alligator. "You ADMIT you did it?"

"Yes," said Camel. "And I really *am* sorry!"

"WHAT?" growled Jackal. "You don't have any excuses?"

"No," said Camel. "I wasn't thinking."

"Well, what about my gorgeous brand new designer clothes?" demanded Vulture.

"They can be fixed," said Camel. "Here, I have a great paint remover."

Camel wiped the paint off Vulture's clothes.

"There!" she said. "Your clothes are good as new."

"What about my lunch?" cried Hippo. "You can't clean my lunch with that stuff!"

Camel held out her lunch box. "Here," she said. "Please take my lunch. It's the *least* I can do. I'm really so sorry!"

Alligator stamped her foot. "Never mind all this!" she sputtered. "It's not enough! Not enough! I want PUNISHMENT! I want REVENGE!"

Alligator lunged at Camel and fell into a pail of red paint.

"Oh, dear!" said Camel. "It's a good thing I have plenty of paint remover!"

"Nyaah!" giggled Nightingale. "What you really need is some Alligator remover!"

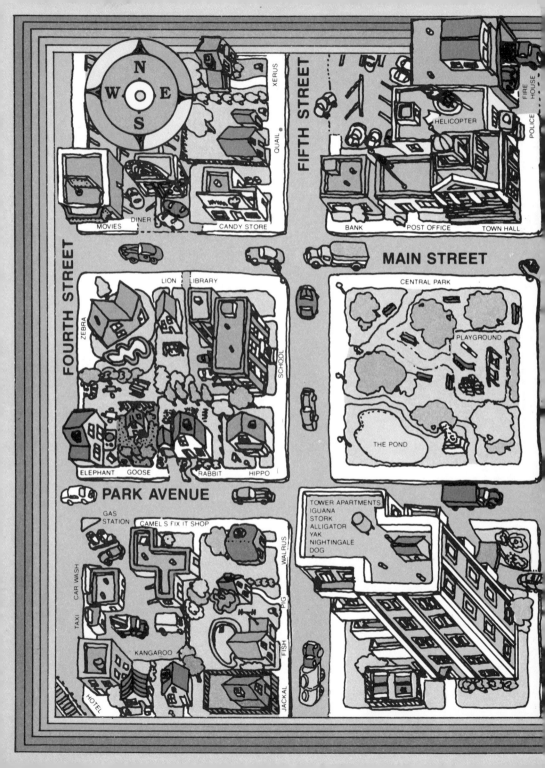